CLUBHOUSE

A SPECIAL THANKS
to Barnaby Dallas for helping co-write *Whitecaps Sets His Sails*. His enthusiasm and passion for the Hubcap Kids' family will always be deeply appreciated.

THIS BOOK IS DEDICATED
to my wife Marianne, for her love and support, and to my daughters, Lauren and Ashley, who are my everything.

Trust in the Lord with all your heart and lean not on your own understanding; in all your ways acknowledge him, and he will make your paths straight.

Proverbs 3:5

Copyright © 1999 by Pat Sunseri
This 1999 edition published by
Broadman & Holman Publishers
Nashville, Tennessee
under arrangement with Ottenheimer Publishers, Inc.
All rights reserved. Printed in Hong Kong.
ISBN 0-8054-2055-X
SB517M L K J I H G F E D C B A

Library of Congress Cataloging-in-Publication Data

Sunseri, Pat, 1955—
    Whitecaps sets his sails / written and illustrated by Pat Sunseri.
        p. cm. — (Hubcap Kids adventures)
    Summary: An encounter with Whitecaps, who is building a ship in a junkyard far from the sea, helps the Hubcap Kids understand the importance of using their talents and following their dreams.
    ISBN 0-8054-2055-X
    [1. Self-realization Fiction. 2. Ships Fiction.]   I. Title.
    II. Series: Sunseri, Pat, 1955— Hubcap kids adventures.
    PZ7.S958273Wh   1999
    [E]—dc21   99-27579
                                                                                      CIP

Scripture quotations are from the Holy Bible, New International Version, copyright 1973, 1978, 1984 by International Bible Society.

Hubcap Kids Adventures

Whitecaps Sets His Sails

story and illustrations by Pat Sunseri

The Hubcap Kids gathered for their weekly clubhouse meeting to play games and practice their favorite hobbies.

Woody stood in the corner building a house with his tools, while Edsel pretended to be a doctor, carefully bandaging Lug's paw. Across the room, Molly Bolt sang one of her favorite songs from the radio into her hairbrush.

Clutch sat at his easel painting the scenic landscape just beyond Hubcap Flats. To his surprise, the landscape had changed dramatically since the Hubcap Kids' last meeting. Clutch sprang from his chair to get a better look.

"Guys! You gotta see this! Someone's building a ship behind Hubcap Flats!" Clutch exclaimed. The Kids rushed to the window. Beyond the fence, half-hidden behind the trees, a wooden mast rose into the sky above the skeleton of a ship's hull. They couldn't believe their eyes!

"That boat's too big for the Hubcap swimming hole," Edsel said.

"Yeah, that ship looks like it should be in the ocean, not at Hubcap Flats," Woody added.

"I'll bet it's old Whitecaps'," Molly Bolt said. "He's always telling stories about his days at sea."

"But there's no ocean around here," Edsel replied.

"Let's go see. Maybe Whitecaps knows something we don't," Clutch suggested.

Sure enough, they found Whitecaps hard at work on the bow of the boat. "What are you doing, Whitecaps?" Clutch asked.

"Building my dream," Whitecaps replied.

"But there's no ocean around here," Molly Bolt said as the other Kids laughed. "Unless there's a flood, your ship will never sail."

Whitecaps looked down at the Kids and said, "Ever since I can remember, I've dreamed of building my own ship and setting sail to the winds of time, going off to faraway lands. Someday, when my ship is finished, though it sits in this old junkyard, I know the winds of time will take my ship full sails and beyond Hubcap Flats."

"Don't you think that's kind of silly?" Clutch asked.

"Not at all. You children can help me build it if you like," Whitecaps replied.

"It's our clubhouse day and we don't want to waste it building a ship that won't even sail," Molly Bolt said. The rest of the Kids nodded in agreement, and they all headed back to the clubhouse.

On their way back to the clubhouse, the Kids passed Mr. Hubcaps painting a workbench he had just finished building for his workshop. Mr. Hubcaps spotted the Kids and asked why they were laughing.

"That boat Whitecaps is building," Molly Bolt said as the other Kids laughed. "He thinks when he's finished he will sail away in it."

"He said it's his dream," Clutch added. "What a crazy dream!"

"It's not so crazy," Mr. Hubcaps said. Then he invited the Kids into his workshop.

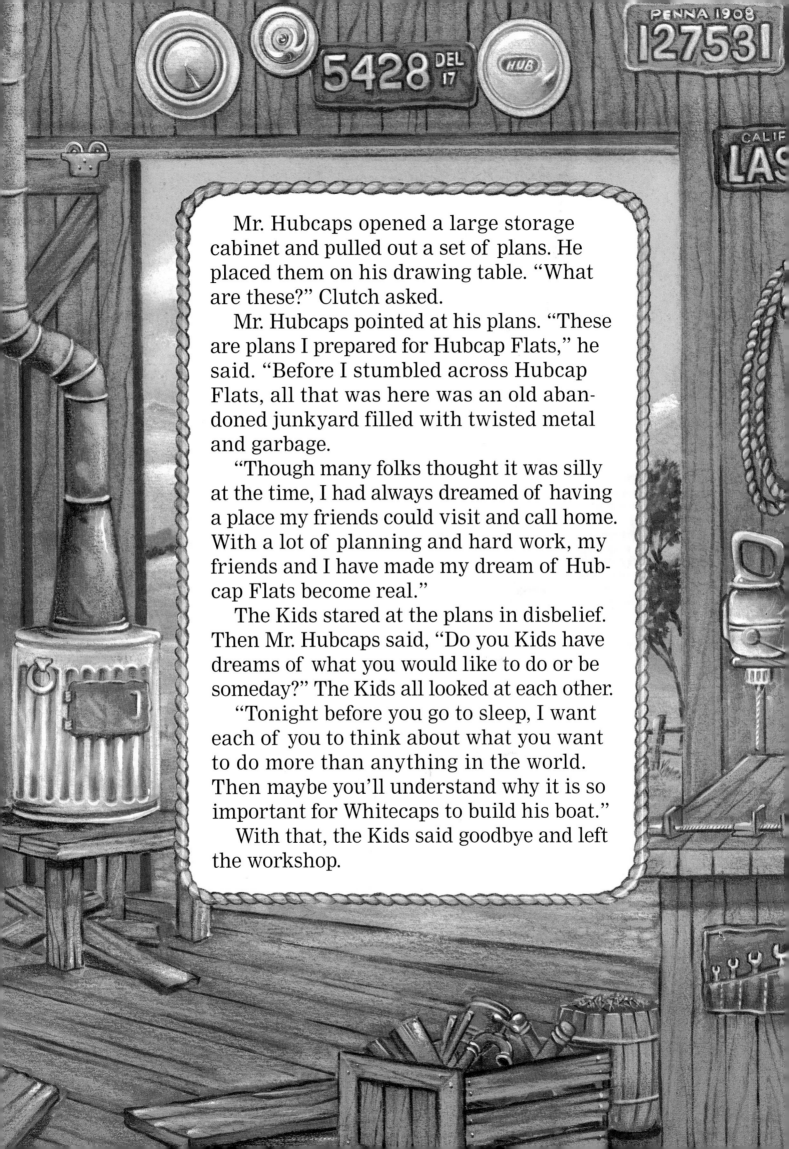

Mr. Hubcaps opened a large storage cabinet and pulled out a set of plans. He placed them on his drawing table. "What are these?" Clutch asked.

Mr. Hubcaps pointed at his plans. "These are plans I prepared for Hubcap Flats," he said. "Before I stumbled across Hubcap Flats, all that was here was an old abandoned junkyard filled with twisted metal and garbage.

"Though many folks thought it was silly at the time, I had always dreamed of having a place my friends could visit and call home. With a lot of planning and hard work, my friends and I have made my dream of Hubcap Flats become real."

The Kids stared at the plans in disbelief. Then Mr. Hubcaps said, "Do you Kids have dreams of what you would like to do or be someday?" The Kids all looked at each other.

"Tonight before you go to sleep, I want each of you to think about what you want to do more than anything in the world. Then maybe you'll understand why it is so important for Whitecaps to build his boat."

With that, the Kids said goodbye and left the workshop.

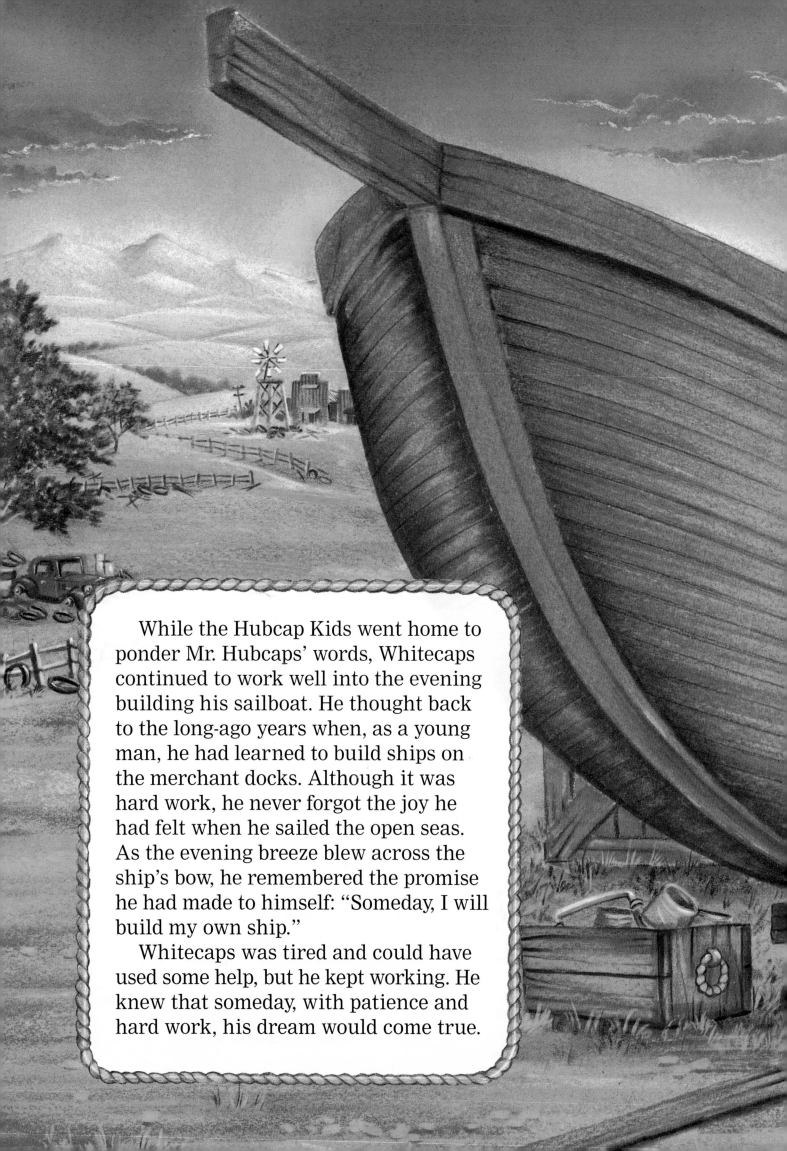

While the Hubcap Kids went home to ponder Mr. Hubcaps' words, Whitecaps continued to work well into the evening building his sailboat. He thought back to the long-ago years when, as a young man, he had learned to build ships on the merchant docks. Although it was hard work, he never forgot the joy he had felt when he sailed the open seas. As the evening breeze blew across the ship's bow, he remembered the promise he had made to himself: "Someday, I will build my own ship."

Whitecaps was tired and could have used some help, but he kept working. He knew that someday, with patience and hard work, his dream would come true.

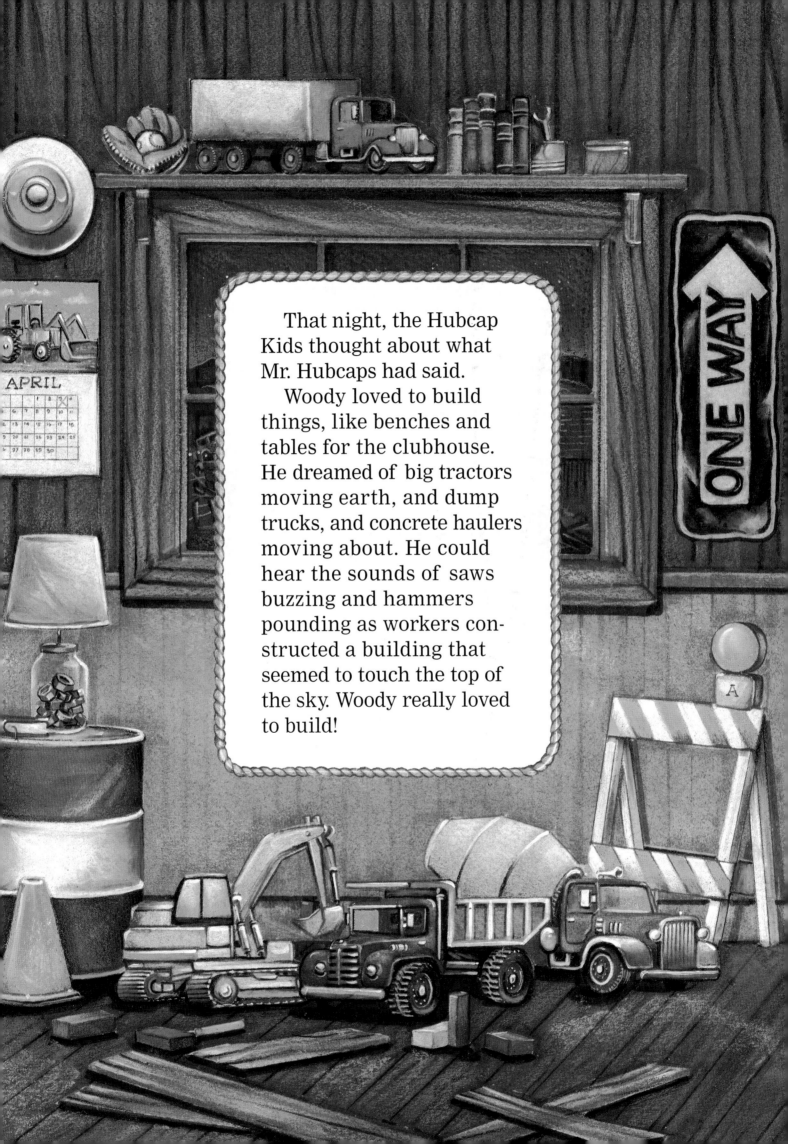

That night, the Hubcap
Kids thought about what
Mr. Hubcaps had said.

Woody loved to build
things, like benches and
tables for the clubhouse.
He dreamed of big tractors
moving earth, and dump
trucks, and concrete haulers
moving about. He could
hear the sounds of saws
buzzing and hammers
pounding as workers con-
structed a building that
seemed to touch the top of
the sky. Woody really loved
to build!

Molly Bolt always sang in the clubhouse for the other Kids, and that night she dreamed of singing and dancing on stage in front of hundreds of people. What a thrill she felt as she twirled gracefully to the music! Molly Bolt loved to perform.

Clutch loved to paint pictures of Hubcap Flats. That night he dreamed of traveling the world, painting beautiful pictures that everyone would come to enjoy. Clutch wanted to be an artist.

Edsel loved animals. That night he dreamed of caring for creatures that were hurt, bandaging their wounds so they would heal and be well again. Animals were very important to Edsel, and he wanted to help them whenever he could.

The next morning the children woke with their dreams fresh in their minds. One by one, they realized that they had dreams just like Mr. Hubcaps and Whitecaps did! They rushed to share their dreams with Mr. Hubcaps.

As he listened intently to each of the children, Mr. Hubcaps could see the excitement in their faces. When the Kids finished, he said, "All of us have hidden talents. You should pay attention to your dreams, and when you know what your dreams and talents are, follow them. And don't be afraid to share your dreams with others," he added. "Often it's your friends who will help you make your dreams come true."

"You're right, Mr. Hubcaps," Molly Bolt exclaimed. "We should all tell Whitecaps our dreams and help him finish his boat!" Mr. Hubcaps smiled to himself as the children rushed to see old Whitecaps.

The Hubcap Kids found Whitecaps hard at work. He gladly accepted their offer to help.

As they all worked together on the boat, the Kids shared their dreams with Whitecaps. Molly Bolt helped make the sails. Woody helped Whitecaps fasten the ship's wheel, and Edsel and Clutch finished painting the boat.

"Whitecaps, we're sorry for making fun of you," Molly Bolt said. The other Kids agreed.

"It's okay," Whitecaps replied. "It took me years to realize my dream. You're young, and if you believe in your dreams and pursue them, someday they may come true."

Whitecaps and the Kids all worked hard throughout the day.

It was late afternoon when they finished. When the Kids looked around for Whitecaps, they found him fast asleep against an old oil drum with a smile on his face. Molly Bolt grabbed a leftover piece of canvas and gently covered him up.

As the Kids stood watching Whitecaps sleep, they talked quietly about their own dreams. Just as they were getting ready to leave, Clutch noticed that the evening clouds had shifted to look almost like a ship in full sails.

"Will you look at that!" Clutch marveled, pointing to the drifting shapes of the clouds. "You know," he mused, "maybe someday Whitecaps really will go full sails beyond Hubcap Flats."